A New Home for Bubbles

By Jo B. Jakar
Illustrated by Mary J. Vyne

ISBN 978-1-66789-444-7

A New Home for Bubbles

To my family, who has always believed in me.
– JBJ

To everyone who has encouraged me to
get my art out there. Here it is!
–MJV

Snap a picture of the QR code to check out some
fun & free learning activities to use with
A New Home for Bubbles!

Bubbles whimpered as Julia picked him up.

"You're going to love it here," she whispered, kissing his head. "And you're going to love your new brother, Porkchop."

Brother? Porkchop? What's a brother? What's a Porkchop? Bubbles wondered. Julia seemed nice. She had already given him plenty of snuggles and kisses, but Bubbles was still unsure about all of this. Questions and worries floated through his mind. After all, for as long as he could remember, his only place in the world was in the tiny cage, next to other dogs in their own tiny cages. *Where am I going now?* he worried.

Julia walked up to a small building and opened the door. When she walked inside, a huge dog pounced on them and covered them in big slobbery kisses.

Why isn't that dog in a cage?! Bubbles wondered.

"Hey, Porkchop!" Julia said, laughing and wiping off the slobber. "I have a surprise! Meet your new brother . . . Bubbles!"

Porkchop twirled around and barked loudly. Julia put Bubbles down. Porkchop immediately buried his nose in Bubbles' fur, sniffing and licking him. Porkchop yipped and twirled and barked over and over again. "Hi! Hi! Hello, new friend!" Porkchop said every time he jumped up.

Now Bubbles had seen other dogs before (he had even sniffed them!), but he had never seen one this big and slobbery and excited and . . . well, loud! Bubbles gave a little whimper and looked at him hesitantly. *Who is this crazy furball? Why is he so excited? And how does he have so much slobber?!*

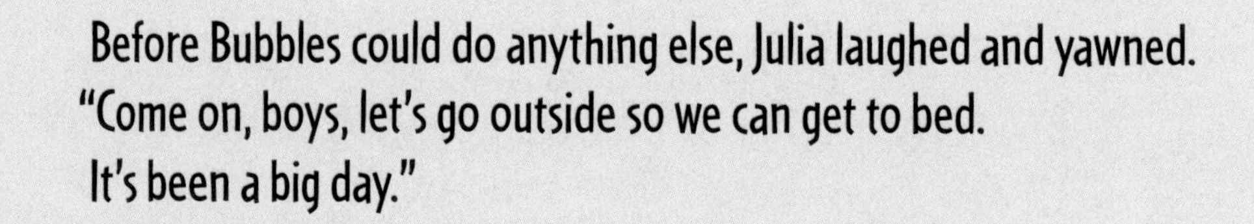

Before Bubbles could do anything else, Julia laughed and yawned. "Come on, boys, let's go outside so we can get to bed. It's been a big day."

The dogs went out in the dark. When they came back inside, Bubbles quietly followed Julia and Porkchop to a large room with a very tall bed. Julia picked him up and placed him on the bed. It was soft, squishy, and so comfortable! Bubbles was unsure what Julia wanted him to do up on this bed. Before Bubbles could sit down, Julia did the craziest thing–she climbed onto the bed with him! Porkchop jumped up clumsily and plopped down right beside him.

This all seemed very strange and new, but Bubbles could barely keep his eyes open. He sat down hesitantly, and before he knew it, he was drifting off to sleep. And for the first time in his life, he wasn't sleeping in a cage.

The next morning, Bubbles woke up to a slobbery kiss. "Pst! Wake up! I have a lot to teach you about life around here!"

Bubbles looked up, confused. All Bubbles could remember doing every day was sitting in a cage and sometimes going for a short walk. *What could he possibly have to teach me?* Bubbles wondered.

Suddenly, a loud sound came blasting out of the tiny rectangle next to Julia's bed. It was lighting up and making a terrible honking sound. Julia moaned and hit the rectangle.

Bubbles whined. *Is something wrong?*

Bubbles looked curiously at the rectangle. It did look pretty magical with the bright light shining from it. He gave it a sniff, and suddenly it started honking again! Bubbles yelped and backed away, his tail between his legs.

"Okay, okay already," Julia grumbled as she grabbed it. She sat up, rubbing her eyes. She gave the dogs a small pat as she stood up and trudged away.

"Okay, the first thing Julia does in the morning is pretty weird," Porkchop explained as they both followed her. They entered a shiny room. Porkchop continued, "This, my friend, is the Land of Water. It's basically just full of water! It's amazing. And very bright."

Bubbles peered around the bright room. There was a counter with a hole in it and a giant white throne. Above the counter was a looking glass on the wall, and in the back of the small room there was a large closet covered with a pretty curtain. There were shiny metal knobs everywhere, glistening in the bright light.

As Bubbles looked around, Julia turned a knob and water started spraying out of a metal tube–right into the hole in the counter! She closed her eyes and started rubbing something all over her face.

"Wh-what is she doing?" Bubbles asked quietly. It was the first question he had been brave enough to ask out loud.

"Oh, it's just a strange dance she does with the water. She rubs stuff all over her face and then washes it off with the water. Then she puts more stuff on her face. When she's done, she smells like flowers," Porkchop replied.

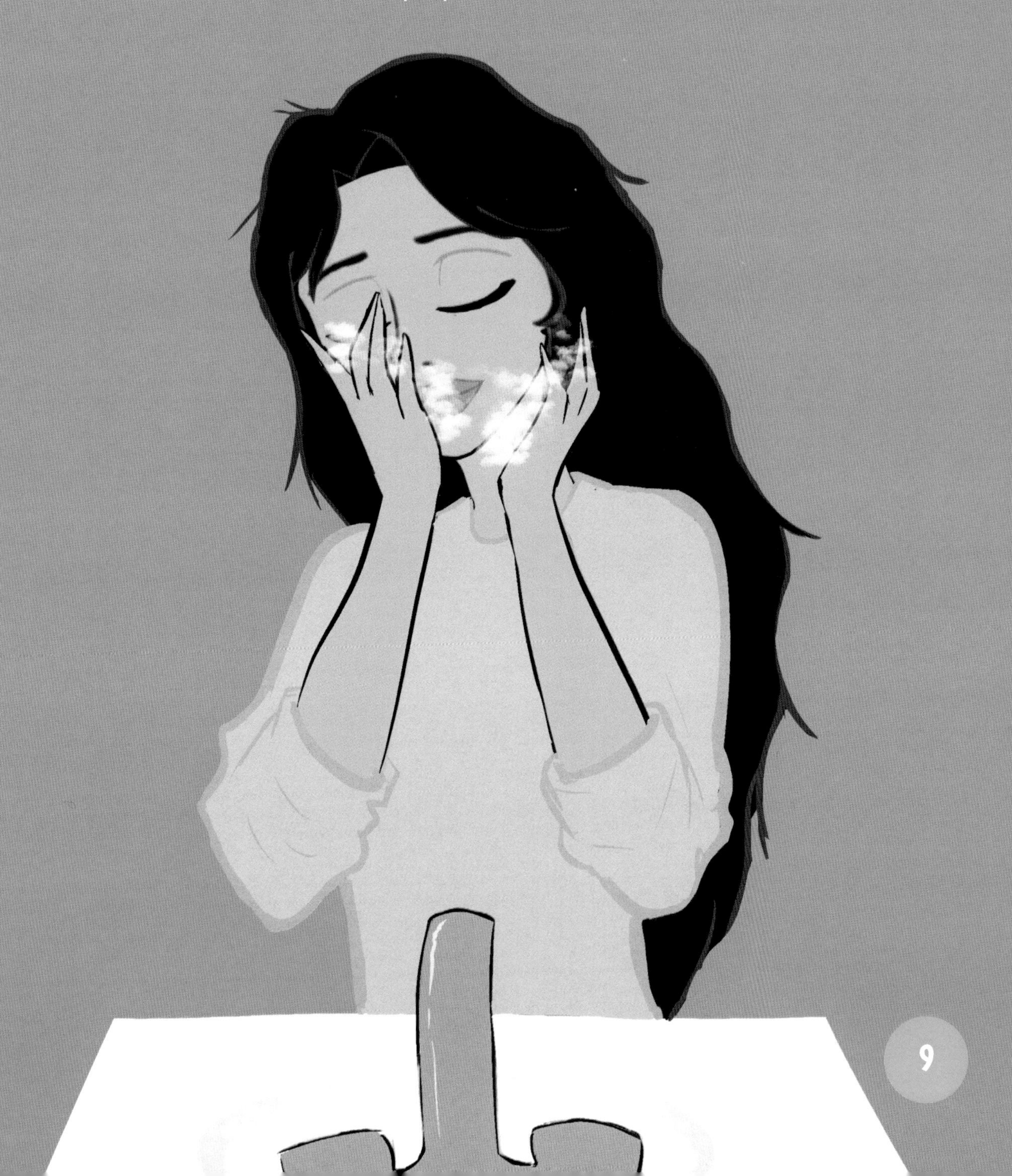

Bubbles could not believe it. He was seeing the strangest things! *A Magical Wake-Up Box? Water on her face? And where did that water come from?!* Bubbles followed Porkchop back to the tall bed.

"By the way, this is called the Land of Snuggles," Porkchop explained, as he jumped on the tall bed again. "We snuggle and sleep here every night! Last night you were pretty tired, so I didn't get a chance to explain that to you."

Just then, they heard the water turn off. They trotted back to Julia.

"Hello!" she said, patting Porkchop and giving Bubbles a kiss. "I'm so glad you have someone to play with now while I'm at work!"

Even though there was a lot of confusing stuff going on, Bubbles had to admit he was starting to feel something new. It felt like a warm smile in his heart.

Julia stood up and turned around. Then she started to do the strangest thing . . . She looked into the looking glass on the wall, and started painting her face! Bubbles was astonished. "What in the world is she doing?" he wondered out loud.

"Oh, she does that every morning," Porkchop replied. "It is kind of weird, but she does it every day!"

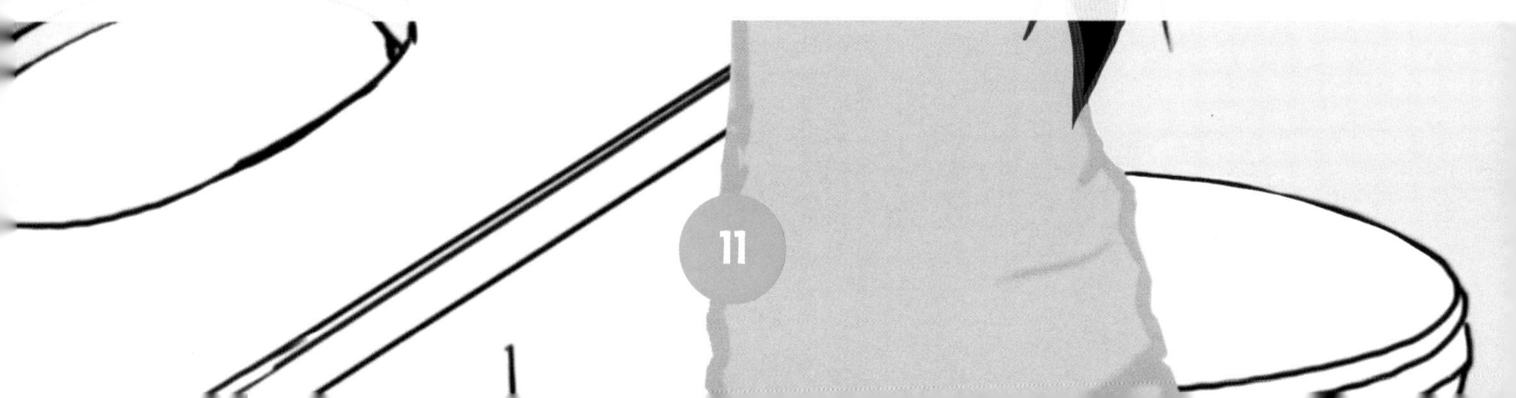

Bubbles just watched, his mouth hanging wide open. When Julia was done painting her face, she took out a stick and put some strong-smelling, paint-like stuff on it. Then she did something even crazier than painting her face—she put the stick in her mouth! She started scrubbing the stick and paint around her teeth, with foam coming out of the sides of her mouth.

"What in the world . . ." Bubbles murmured.

Suddenly, she spat the foam out!

"I don't know why she does that. It makes her breath smell pretty weird," Porkchop said. "Like I said, she does some strange stuff."

Bubbles' mind raced with questions, but before he could decide which one to ask first, Julia walked out and smiled at the dogs. "Ready to go potty, boys?"

"What's a potty?" Bubbles whispered, but Porkchop didn't hear him. He was already racing to the door.

Bubbles slowly followed Porkchop to the door. When Julia opened it, Porkchop bolted out and Bubbles peered outside. He could barely believe his eyes. Last night it had been dark when they came out here. Now that the sun was up, he could see . . . and it was the most beautiful place in the whole world!

There were trees, grass, flowers, and bushes. And surrounding all of this were tall white sticks sticking out of the ground. "Come on! Time to go potty!" Porkchop said. Bubbles quickly figured out what that meant from Porkchop's example.

Bubbles did his business and was ready to explore this beautiful playground, but all too soon Julia was calling them to come back inside. Bubbles wanted to stay and explore, but he didn't want to disobey Julia. After all, she did invite him to this magical place. He was beginning to think he may actually want to stay.

“Get ready for some fun,” Porkchop said, trotting back inside with Bubbles. “You’re going to love it here. I used to spend my days all alone. But now I have you! We can play, play, play, play all day!”

This furball was pretty goofy, but Bubbles couldn’t help but smile at his excitement . . . it did sound like fun to play all day!

As they walked back inside, Bubbles sniffed a strong and strange smell. When he spotted where it was coming from, he watched Julia pour dark liquid into a cup with a handle. Steam rose from the cup. She took a sip. Bubbles couldn't imagine sipping something that smelled so awful!

"What is that?" Bubbles whispered to Porkchop.

"Oh, that?" Porkchop answered. "I'm not sure, but she has it every day. One time I snuck a lick when she wasn't looking because I was curious. It smells awful, but by the way she drinks it everyday, I thought it must be tasty. But, no, I was wrong. It is nasty! Don't ever try it. Trust me. Plus it's way too hot."

Bubbles nodded, thankful for the very useful information.

"But she does have some round bread with a hole in the middle," Porkchop continued. "Now that is delicious. And the white goo she puts on it is so tasty! Sometimes she lets me have her last bite, and it is so good! I call it Hole Bread with Goo." Slobber started dripping out of the sides of Porkchop's mouth as he explained.

Just then a round piece of bread with a hole in the middle popped out of a machine. Julia spread the white goo on it and started to munch away. Bubbles stared up at her, wishing his hardest he would get a bite of the Hole Bread and Goo. It sounded like the most delicious thing in the world!

Julia looked down at him and smiled. She tossed the last two bites to the two dogs. Bubbles gulped his bite down just like Porkchop. Porkchop was right–it was delicious!

"Wow! I never knew so many amazingly strange things even existed!" Bubbles said, smiling.

Porkchop gave him a lick. "Oh just wait till you see the rest! I'll show you once Julia leaves." Porkchop wagged his tail so hard, he knocked over a small plant on the floor. Julia bent to pick it up. As he watched her, Bubbles couldn't help but wonder, *Why would she ever leave this magical land?*

"All right, boys, I'm going to work!" Julia said, shaking a jingle toy. She patted them both on the head and was out the door.

“Alright, buddy! She’s gone! I have more to show you!” And with that, Porkchop trotted back to the Land of Water.

Bubbles gave a little whine. He wished Julia would come back to play, but he slowly turned to meet Porkchop. After seeing their playground outside, he guessed there was more fun in store for the rest of the day!

When he entered the Land of Water, Porkchop was already talking. "Okay, first thing, this throne has the best water in it!" And with that, he stuck his head in the throne and started lapping up water. “Mmm . . . delicious! Now it’s your turn! We can only drink out of the throne when Julia is gone. For some reason, she doesn’t want us to do it. So enjoy it now!”

Bubbles was hesitant to stick his head into a giant throne. *Why does she have a throne with water, anyway?* he couldn't help but wonder. When he got up to the throne, he realized he couldn't reach.

"Aw, that's too bad," Porkchop said. "Well, you'll grow into it. It's something you can look forward to when you get bigger!"

Bubbles nodded. *Will I still be here when I'm bigger?* he wondered to himself. Drinking out of a throne seemed strange, but still pretty interesting. And this crazy furball seemed nice, even if he was a little silly. Plus he really liked Julia. He hoped she would come back soon.

Before Bubbles could think too much, Porkchop yipped and said, "Okay now to the Land of Clothes!" He still had throne water dripping out of his mouth. "Let's go!"

And with that, Bubbles followed Porkchop to another room. Porkchop gently nudged the door with his nose and revealed a room unlike anything Bubbles had ever seen before. It was small, but colorful and full. Two giant machines sat in the corner, and there were piles of clothes everywhere. Some were hanging on hooks, some were scattered on the floor, and some were overflowing from a large basket.

Bubbles looked around the colorful room, curious, but confused yet again.

"Sometimes I come in here and snuggle with all of these clothes. They're cozy and they smell good! I especially like these little foot-shaped ones," Porkchop said, nudging one over to Bubbles.

Bubbles took a sniff. Porkchop was right—it did smell yummy! Before he knew it, Bubbles was jumping into a basket of clothes and burying his nose in it, trying to get a good snuggle. They all smelled like Julia, which made him miss her even more. But he had to admit, he was having fun with Porkchop.

The two dogs played in the clothes room for a long time, even taking a break for a nap—right on top of the pile of clothes.

When they woke up, Porkchop chuckled. "We can come back to play in the Land of Clothes, but I have something else to show you! Come on!"

Porkchop and Bubbles stretched, then trotted back to the Land of Snuggles. Porkchop nudged open another door. Inside, endless colorful clothes hung on a rod. But the best part was the toys on the floor.

Several pairs of the most beautiful chew toys Bubbles had ever seen were neatly organized on the floor. Tall ones, flat ones, leather ones, colorful ones, ones with straps . . . and they all smelled delicious! The best part was that there were two of each of the remarkable toys–one stacked right next to its twin!

Before Bubbles could stop himself, he pounced on one particularly yummy-smelling pair of toys. They were bright and colorful and had strings all the way up with a delicious bow.

"No!" Porkchop shouted, quickly nudging the chew toy out of his mouth. "Now, Julia does not like when we mess things up in here, so we have to be very careful," Porkchop explained. "These are only for us to look at and sniff. I know, it is very hard to resist chewing on them. But she gets very upset if I chew on them. So just give it a big sniff and maybe even a small lick. But she can never know we were in here. One time I accidentally got carried away and chewed up one of the toys. She was not happy!"

Bubbles nodded. He was disappointed he couldn't chew more on the delicious toy, but he didn't want to upset Julia. After all these new discoveries and getting to know his new furball friend, he knew he wanted to stay here forever! He nudged the toy back right next to its partner and was about to sniff the tall one when, suddenly, there was a jingle at the door.

"Quick! She's home!" Porkchop yipped.

Quickly, they nudged the toys back. At that moment, they heard Julia.

"Boys! I'm home!"

Porkchop yelped and scurried to the door to greet her, Bubbles close behind.

"Hi, boys! Did you have a good day together?" Julia asked as she smiled and scratched their heads. Porkchop barked and wagged his tail.

Bubbles gave a small yip. He just hoped Julia would let him stay so that he could play in this wonderful place forever.

Julia let the dogs outside to do their business. It seemed like no time had passed when Julia came to the door, shouting, "Porkchop! Bubbles! Dinner!"

The dogs ran inside to find two bowls of dog food on the floor. Bubbles hadn't realized how hungry he was! He dug in, enjoying his feast with his new best buddy.

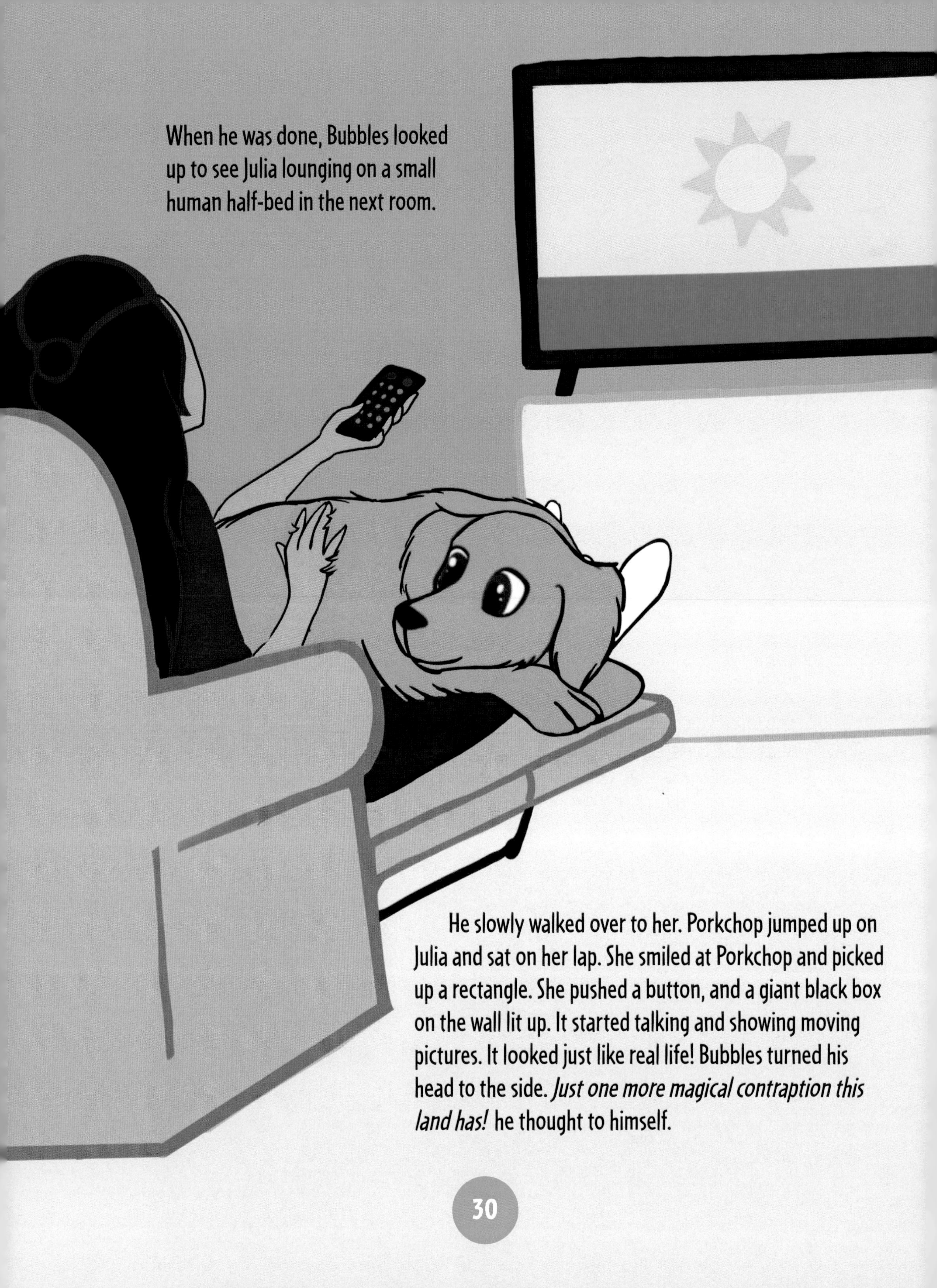

When he was done, Bubbles looked up to see Julia lounging on a small human half-bed in the next room.

He slowly walked over to her. Porkchop jumped up on Julia and sat on her lap. She smiled at Porkchop and picked up a rectangle. She pushed a button, and a giant black box on the wall lit up. It started talking and showing moving pictures. It looked just like real life! Bubbles turned his head to the side. *Just one more magical contraption this land has!* he thought to himself.

Bubbles glanced back over at Julia and Porkchop. He wanted to join in the snuggles, so he inched closer and looked up. He wasn't sure what he should do next.

Julia laughed. "Oh, you are getting so good at showing me those puppy eyes!" she said. Julia picked him up and he snuggled up next to them.

Bubbles closed his eyes, full of happiness.

"I hope you like your new home," Julia whispered, as she scratched his belly and kissed his head.

Bubbles licked Julia's hand and looked at Porkchop. *I love my new home,* Bubbles thought.

And with that, he dozed off.

Snuggled up with his new family.

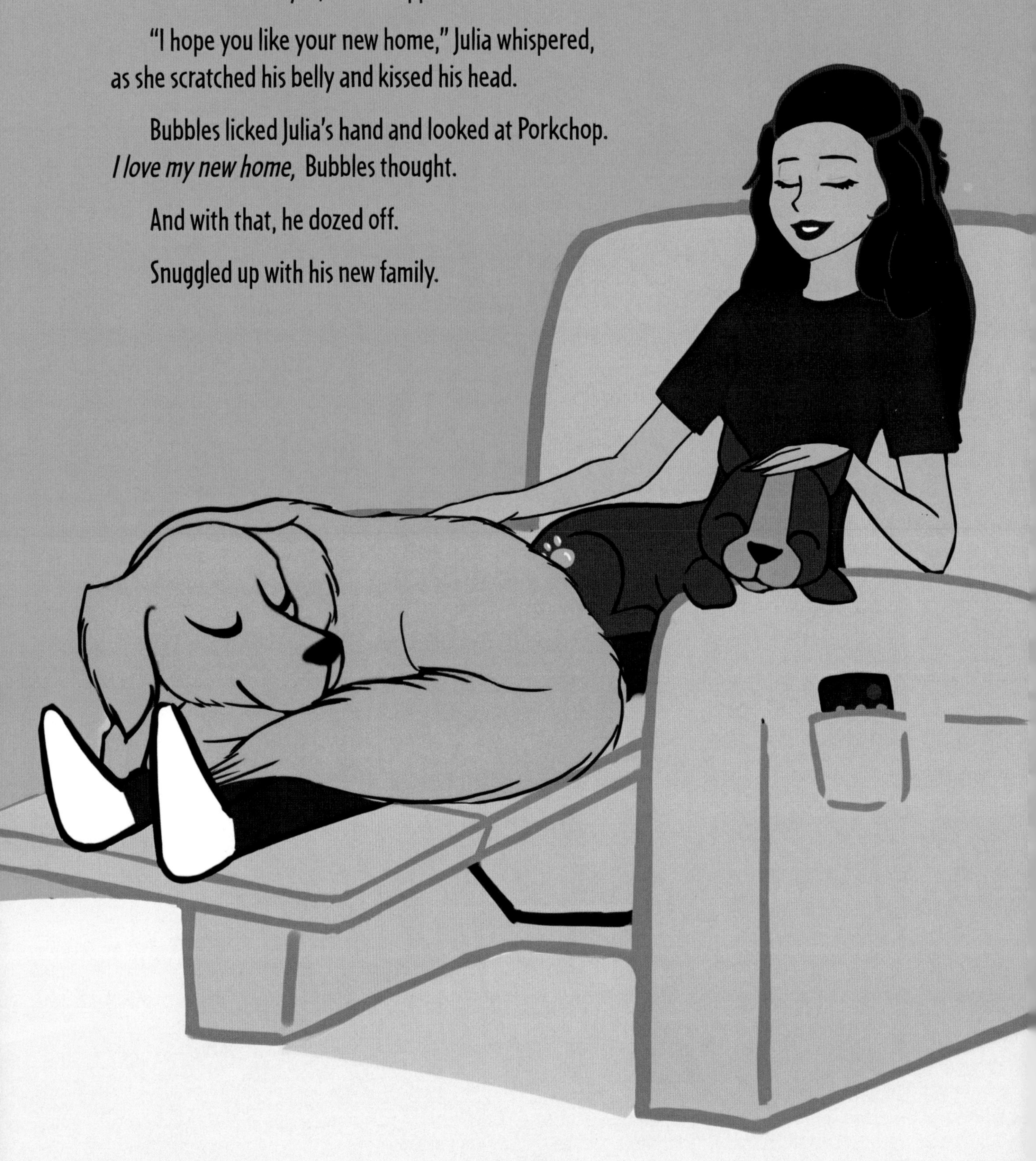

About the Author

Jo B. Jakar has always loved to get lost in a good book. Her passion for reading drove her instruction during her time as a literacy teacher. While in the classroom, Jo learned the importance of using good books as the foundation for passionate, lifelong learning.

Now Jo is a stay-at-home mom for her beautiful children. She firmly believes that reading promotes learning in the most wonderful way. She hopes to use her God-given gifts to create tools for young learners to ignite a love for reading and learning. Jo enjoys being with her family, exploring outside, and baking.

About the Illustrator

Mary J. Vyne has been an artist since the day she was born. She has always been able to create beauty from simplicity in all walks of life. During the day she works as a barber; she loves to use her creative side with her clients' hair to help them feel their absolute best. After hours, Mary's passion is creating her own art - particularly sketching and watercolor. She also loves reading, music, and her pets.